WARNING

ENTER AT YOUR OWN RISK

NOT RESPONSIBLE FOR INJURIES / ACCIDENTS OF ANY KIND

SPEED
LIMIT
25

CRYSTAL LAKE
ENTERTAINMENT

CAUTION

INCIDENT ON AND OFF A MOUNTAIN ROAD

Written by
Joe R. Lansdale

Illustrated by
Ted DiLucia

SPEED
LIMIT
55

Text copyright © 2023 by Joe R. Lansdale
Illustrations copyright © 2023 by Ted DiLucia
All rights reserved.
Published by Crystal Lake Entertainment:

Library of Congress Cataloging-in-Publication Data

Lansdale, Joe R.
Incident On and Off a Mountain Road / by Joe R. Lansdale

Summary: On the road to her newly found freedom, a young woman encounters a backwoods serial killer driven by bloodlust and the light of the moon. In order to secure her survival, the young woman must use her quick wit and cunning ingenuity to escape safe and untouched.

ISBN 978-1-957133-35-5

10 9 8 7 6 5 4 3 2 1

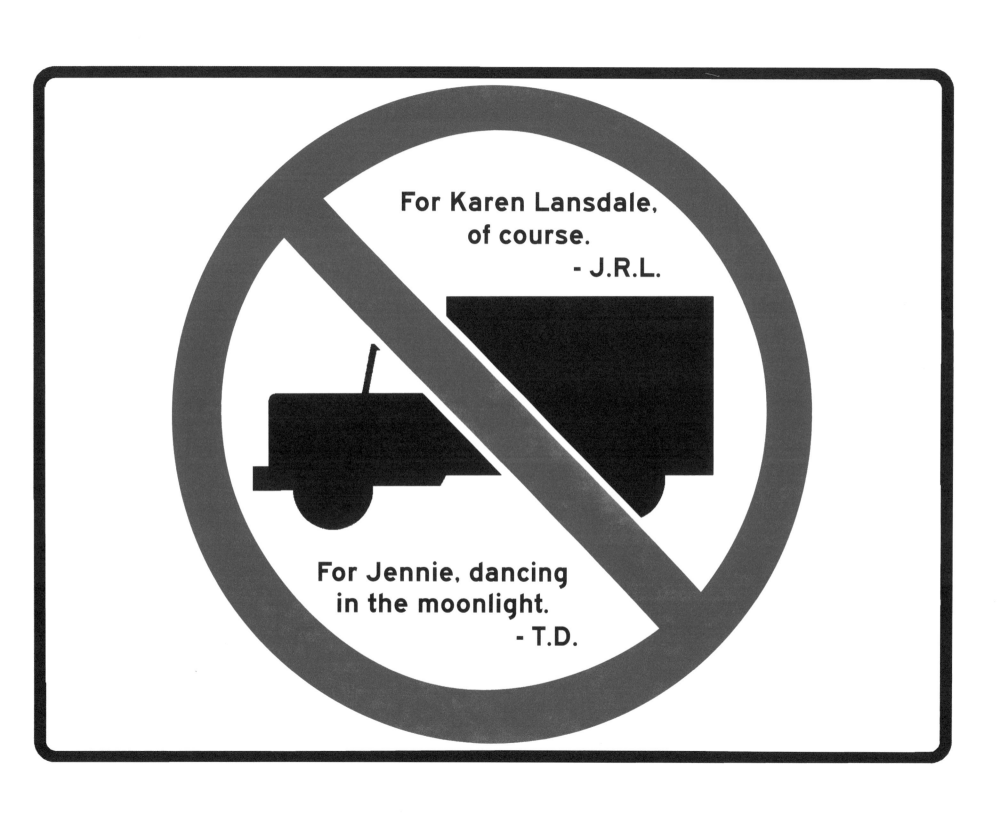

For Karen Lansdale,
of course.
- J.R.L.

For Jennie, dancing
in the moonlight.
- T.D.

SLOW DOWN
CHILDREN PLAYING
A word from horror master DON COSCARELLI

An illustrated version of one of Joe R. Lansdale's books is long overdue. What originally drew me to Joe's work was that, unlike many authors, his writing style paints vivid imagery in one's mind. I remember the very first Lansdale book I read, The Drive In, and thinking at the time that it seemed to be written for the movies. Being a visual storyteller myself, Joe's work seemed like a perfect match for me.

Most people don't know that when I acquired the rights to transform Joe's classic novella Bubba Ho-tep into a film, at the same time I also made a deal for the rights to his short story Incident On and Off a Mountain Road. With the strong female lead role and the requisite action and horror elements I felt it might be possible to get funding for a feature film based on it. Unfortunately, try as I might, I was never able to find a way to lengthen the story to feature length and the rights ultimately lapsed. A few years later the talented horror writer and director Mick Garris pitched me on joining up with him on his Masters of Horror TV series for Showtime with the central concept of producing a one-hour horror film of anything I wanted to do. Of course Joe and Incident On and Off a Mountain Road immediately popped into my mind and literally within days I was hard at work creating an adaptation of it in collaboration with the acclaimed Austin author, Stephen Romano.

What originally struck me about Joe's terrific story was how it turned the stereotypical "damsel in distress" story on its head. We've seen that cliched yarn time and time again in books and horror movies. Yet Joe toys with the reader, allowing them to believe that he's put a new spin on the old trope, with Ellen's boyfriend Bruce coming to her from the past to save the day in the present. Well, Bruce's teachings do seem to save the day for Ellen until Joe unleashes the mother of all sucker punches, which I like to think would have made O. Henry proud.

Ted DiLucia has done a masterful job of illustrating this book and capturing the mystery and horror of Incident On and Off a Mountain Road. His artwork is moving and cinematic in its own right and a worthy addition to Joe's classic short story. Ted's use of collage elements creates art that is at once cool and elegant, yet at the same time frightening and freaky. In taking on this project, Ted may find out that he's made himself a deal with the devil. Joe has an immense catalog of brilliant and imaginative stories and novels. This new edition of Incident On and Off a Mountain Road turned out so well, Ted just may find himself illustrating Joe R. Lansdale books for years to come. The Magic Wagon? The Nightrunners? Zeppelin's West? I certainly hope so!

FEB 7 2023

DEER 🦌 XING

BEWARE: word from the curator of the masters MICK GARRIS

Once upon a time, I hosted a series of dinners for directors of horror films. It wasn't a club or a union or a network or anything beyond just a small group of friends who work in the same field getting together to hang out and share war stories. The food and drink were secondary to just a friendly gathering. There were twelve people at that first dinner, including John Carpenter, Guillermo del Toro, Stuart Gordon, William Malone, Joe Dante, John Landis, and, most importantly for readers of this book, Don Coscarelli. It was held at a restaurant in Sherman Oaks, California, where no one in the restaurant knew that the most sinister minds in horror cinema were gathered at a table amongst them. There were many more dinners over the years that followed, and each one had more attendees. Word started to spread among the genre creators, and it started to get pretty unwieldy. By the time we did our last one (so far), the number had climbed to 35. One of the topics of conversation was how we as horror genre directors were so rarely able to make the films we wanted to make, the way we wanted to make them. So I got this idea… What if the inmates ran the asylum?

So MASTERS OF HORROR was born, with the brightest lights in the horror field were offered the ability to make their movies—on a limited schedule, without much money—but without studio or network interference! And you know what? Anchor Bay, the first company we pitched it to, said, "how much, and when can you start?" And we were off and running. Though it was not the first episode we shot (that distinction goes to John Landis's DEER WOMAN) we decided to debut the series with Coscarelli's brilliant adaptation of Joe Lansdale's terrifying INCIDENT ON AND OFF A MOUNTAIN ROAD, because we felt it offered everything the horror audience we were seeking was looking for.

Lansdale tells his stories with highly visual prose. You can see the horrifying visage of Moonface in your mind's eye. The color and atmosphere and characters are cinematic to begin with, and with a proven collaborator like Don (see their previous film of BUBBA HO-TEP, and you'll understand), theirs was a match made in hell. In fact, Dark Horse toyed with a couple issues of a MASTERS OF HORROR comic, including an adaptation of INCIDENT, but it never went anywhere.

But now, in all its glory, you hold in your hands (or on your screen) an all-new graphic adaptation of Lansdale's story, newly and fully illustrated by the very talented Ted DiLucia. It's a new way to take in this story, blending the text and artwork that feels like Coscarelli's film adaptation. It is suspenseful and gnarly and peppered with Lansdale's dark red humor; and Joe always swings left when you are expecting him to hit right. So… this is a movie, but you just turn the pages.

So take a trip into that Texas twilight… but remember… beware the Moon(face).

MAR 6 2023

WRONG

INCIDENT ON AND OFF
A MOUNTAIN ROAD

WAY

When Ellen came to the moonlit mountain curve, her thoughts, which had been adrift with her problems, grounded, and she was suddenly aware that she was driving much too fast. The sign said curve: 30 mph, and she was doing fifty. She knew too that slamming on the brakes was the wrong move, so she optioned to keep her speed and fight the curve and make it, and she thought she could.

The moonlight was strong, so visibility was high, and she knew her Chevy was in good shape, easy to handle, and she was a good driver. But as she negotiated the curve a blue Buick seemed to grow out of the ground in front of her. It was parked on the shoulder of the road, at the peak of the curve, its nose sticking out a foot too far, its rear end against the moon-wet, silver railing that separated the curve from a mountainous plunge.

Had she been going an appropriate speed, missing the Buick wouldn't have been a problem, but at her speed she was swinging too far right, directly in line with it, and was forced, after all, to use her brakes. When she did, the back wheels slid and the brakes groaned and the front of the Chevy hit the Buick, and there was a sound like an explosion and then for a dizzy instant she felt as if she were in the tumblers of a dryer.

Through the windshield came: Moonlight. Blackness. Moonlight.

One high bounce and a tight roll, and the Chevy came to rest upright with the engine dead, the right side flush against the railing. Another inch of jump or greater impact against the rail, and the Chevy would have gone over.

Ellen felt a sharp pain in her leg and reached down to discover that during the tumble she had banged it against something, probably the gear shift, and had ripped her stocking and her flesh. Blood was trickling into her shoe. Probing her leg cautiously with the tips of her fingers, she determined the wound wasn't bad and that all other body parts were operative. She unfastened her seat belt, and as a matter of habit, located her purse and slipped its strap over her shoulder. She got out of the Chevy feeling wobbly, eased around front of it and saw the hood and bumper and roof were crumpled.

A wisp of radiator steam hissed from beneath the wadded hood, rose into the moonlight and dissolved. She turned her attentions to the Buick. Its tail end was now turned to her, and as she edged alongside it, she saw the front left side had been badly damaged. Fearful of what she might see, she glanced inside.

The moonlight shone through the rear windshield bright as a spotlight and revealed no one, but the back seat was slick with something dark and wet and there was plenty of it. A foul scent seeped out of a partially rolled down back window. It was a hot coppery smell that gnawed at her nostrils and ached her stomach.

God, someone had been hurt. Maybe thrown free of the car, or perhaps they had gotten out and crawled off. But when? She and the Chevy had been airborne for only a moment, and she had gotten out of the vehicle instants after it ceased to roll. Surely she would have seen someone get out of the Buick, and if they had been thrown free by the collision, wouldn't at least one of the Buick's doors be open? If it had whipped back and closed, it seemed unlikely that it would be locked, and all the doors of the Buick were locked, and all the glass was intact, and only on her side was it rolled down, and only a crack.

Enough for the smell of the blood to escape, not enough for a person to slip through unless they were thin and flexible as a feather.

On the other side of the Buick, on the ground, between the back door and the railing, there were drag marks and a thick swath of blood, and another swath on the top of the railing; it glowed there in the moonlight as if it were molasses laced with radioactivity.

Ellen moved cautiously to the railing and peered over.

No one lay mangled and bleeding and oozing their guts. The ground was not as precarious there as she expected it. It was pebbly and sloped out gradually and there was a trail going down it. The trail twisted slightly and as it deepened the foliage grew denser on either side of it. Finally it curlicued its way into the dark thicket of a forest below, and from the forest, hot on the wind, came the strong turpentine tang of pines and something less fresh and not as easily identifiable.

Now she saw someone moving down there, floating up from the forest like an apparition; a white face split by silver--braces, perhaps. She could tell from the way this someone moved that it was a man. She watched as he climbed the Incident On and Off a Mountain Road 177 trail and came within examination range. He seemed to be surveying her as carefully as she was surveying him.

Could this be the driver of the Buick?

As he came nearer Ellen discovered she could not identify the expression he wore. It was neither joy or anger or fear or exhaustion or pain. It was somehow all and none of these.

When he was ten feet away, still looking up, that same odd expression on his face, she could hear him breathing. He was breathing with exertion, but not to the extent she thought him tired or injured. It was the sound of someone who had been about busy work.

She yelled down, "Are you injured?"

He turned his head quizzically, like a dog trying to make sense of a command, and it occurred to Ellen that he might be knocked about in the head enough to be disoriented.

"I'm the one who ran into your car," she said. "Are you all right?"

His expression changed then, and it was most certainly identifiable this time. He was surprised and angry. He came up the trail quickly, took hold of the top railing, his fingers going into the blood there, and vaulted over and onto the gravel.

Ellen stepped back out of his way and watched him from a distance. The guy made her nervous. Even close up, he looked l ike some kind of spook.

He eyed her briefly, glanced at the Chevy, turned to look at the Buick.

"It was my fault," Ellen said.

He didn't reply, but returned his attention to her and continued to cock his head in that curious dog sort of way.

Ellen noticed that one of his shirt sleeves was stained with blood, and that there was blood on the knees of his pants, but he didn't act as if he were hurt in any way. He reached into his pants pocket and pulled out something and made a move with his wrist. Out flicked a lock-blade knife. The thin edge of it sucked up the moonlight and spat it out in a silver spray that fanned wide when he held it before him and jiggled it like a man working a stubborn key into a lock. He advanced toward her, and as he came, his lips split and pulled back at the corners, exposing, not braces, but metal-capped teeth that matched the sparkle of his blade.

It occurred to her that she could bolt for the Chevy, but in the same mental flash of lightning, it occurred to her she wouldn't make it.

Ellen threw herself over the railing, and as she leapt, she saw out of the corner of her eye, the knife slashing the place she had occupied, catching moonbeams and throwing them away. Then the blade was out of her view and she hit on her stomach and skidded onto the narrow trail, slid downward, feet first.

The gravel and roots tore at the front of her dress and ripped through her nylons and gouged her flesh. She cried out in pain and her sliding gained speed. Lifting her chin, she saw that the man was climbing over the railing and coming after her at a stumbling run, the knife held before him like a wand.

Her sliding stopped, and she pushed off with her hands to make it start again, not knowing if this was the thing to do or not, since the trail inclined sharply on her right side, and should she skid only slightly in that direction, she could hurtle off into blackness. But somehow she kept slithering along the trail and even spun around a corner and stopped with her head facing downward, her purse practically in her teeth.

She got up then, without looking back, and began to run into the woods, the purse beating at her side. She moved as far away from the trail as she could, fighting limbs that conspired to hit her across the face or hold her, vines and bushes that tried to tie her feet or trip her.

Behind her, she could hear the man coming after her, breathing heavily now, not really winded, but hurrying. For the first time in months, she was grateful for Bruce and his survivalist insanity. His passion to be in shape and for her to be in shape with him was paying off. All that jogging had given her the lungs of an ox and strengthened her legs and ankles. A line from one of Bruce's survivalist books came to her: Do the unexpected.

She found a trail amongst the pines, and followed it, then, abruptly broke from it and went back into the thicket. It was harder going, but she assumed her pursuer would expect her to follow a trail.

The pines became so thick she got down on her hands and knees and began to crawl. It was easier to get through that way. After a moment, she stopped scuttling and eased her back against one of the pines and sat and listened. She felt reasonably well hidden, as the boughs of the pines grew low and drooped to the ground. She took several deep breaths, holding each for a long moment. Gradually, she began breathing normally. Above her, from the direction of the trail, she could hear the man running, coming nearer. She held her breath.

The running paused a couple of times, and she could imagine the man, his strange, pale face turning from side to side, as he tried to determine what had happened to her. The sound of running started again and the man moved on down the trail.

Ellen considered easing out and starting back up the trail, making her way to her car and driving off. Damaged as it was, she felt it would still run, but she was reluctant to leave her hiding place and step into the moonlight.

Still, it seemed a better plan than waiting. If she didn't do something, the man could always go back topside himself and wait for her. The woods, covering acres and acres of land below and beyond, would take her days to get through, and without food and water and knowledge of the geography, she might never make it, could end up going in circles for days.

Bruce and his survivalist credos came back to her. She remembered something he had said to one of his self-defense classes, a bunch of rednecks hoping and praying for a commie take-over so they could show their stuff. He had told them: "Utilize what's at hand. Size up what you have with you and how it can be put to use."

All right, she thought. All right, Brucey, you sonofabitch. I'll see what's at hand.

One thing she knew she had for sure was a little flashlight. It wasn't much, but it would serve for her to check out the contents of her purse. She located it easily, and without withdrawing it from her purse, turned it on and held the open purse close to her face to see what was inside. Before she actually found it, she thought of her nail file kit. Besides the little bottle of nail polish remover, there was an emery board and two metal files. The files were the ticket. They might serve as weapons; they weren't much, but they were something.

She also carried a very small pair of nail scissors, independent of the kit, the points of the scissors being less than a quarter inch. That wouldn't be worth much, but she took note of it and mentally catalogued it. She found the nail kit, turned off the flash and removed one of the files and returned the rest of the kit to her purse. She held the file tightly, made a little jabbing motion with it. It seemed so light and thin and insignificant. She had been absently carrying her purse on one shoulder, and now to make sure she didn't lose it, she placed the strap over her neck and slid her arm through.

Clenching the nail file, she moved on hands and knees beneath the pine boughs and poked her head out into the clearing of the trail. She glanced down it first, and there, not ten yards from her, looking up the trail, holding his knife by his side, was the man. The moonlight lay cold on his face and the shadows of the wind-blown boughs fell across him and wavered. It seemed as if she were leaning over a pool and staring down into the water and seeing him at the bottom of it, or perhaps his reflection on the face of the pool.

She realized instantly that he had gone down the trail a ways, became suspicious of her ability to disappear so quickly, and had turned to judge where she might have gone. And, as if in answer to the question, she poked her head into view.

They remained frozen for a moment, then the man took a step up the trail, and just as he began to run, Ellen went backwards into the pines on her hands and knees.

She had gone less than ten feet when she ran up against a thick limb that lay close to the ground and was preventing her passage. She got down on her belly and squirmed beneath it, and as she was pulling her head under, she saw Moon Face crawling into the thicket, making good time; time made better, when he lunged suddenly and covered half the space between them, the knife
missing her by fractions.

Ellen jerked back and felt her feet falling away from her. She let go of the file and grabbed out for the limb and it bent way back and down with her weight. It lowered her enough for her feet to touch ground. Relieved, she realized she had fallen into a wash made by erosion, not off the edge of the mountain. Above her, gathered in shadows and stray strands of moonlight that showed through the pine boughs, was the man. His metal-tipped teeth caught a moonbeam and twinkled. He placed a hand on the limb she held, as if to lower himself, and she let go of it.

The limb whispered away from her and hit him full in the face and knocked him back. Ellen didn't bother to scrutinize the damage. Turning, she saw that the wash ended in a slope and that the slope was thick with trees growing out like great, feathered spears thrown into the side of the mountain. She started down, letting the slant carry her, grasping limbs and tree trunks to slow her descent and keep her balance. She could hear the man climbing down and pursuing her, but she didn't bother to turn and look. Below she could see the incline was becoming steeper, and if she continued, it would be almost straight up and down with nothing but the trees for support, and to move from one to the other, she would have to drop, chimpanzee-like, from limb to limb. Not a pleasant thought.

Her only consolation was that the trees to her right, veering back up the mountain, were thick as cancer cells. She took off in that direction, going wide, and began plodding upwards again, trying to regain the concealment of the forest. She chanced a look behind her before entering the pines, and saw that the man, who she had come to think of as Moon Face, was some distance away.

Weaving through a mass of trees, she integrated herself into the forest, and as she went the limbs began to grow closer to the ground and the trees became so thick they twisted together like pipe cleaners. She got down on her hands and knees and crawled between limbs and around tree trunks and tried to lose herself among them.

To follow her, Moon Face had to do the same thing, and at first she heard him behind her, but after a while, there were only the sounds she was making.

She paused and listened.

Nothing.

Glancing the way she had come, she saw the intertwining limbs she had crawled under mixed with penetrating moonbeams, heard the short bursts of her breath and the beating of her heart, but detected no evidence of Moon Face. She decided the head start she had, all the weaving she had done, the cover of the pines, had confused him, at least temporarily. It occurred to her that if she had stopped to listen, he might have done the same, and she wondered if he could hear the pounding of her heart. She took a deep breath and held it and let it out slowly through her nose, did it again.

She was breathing more normally now, and her heart, though still hammering furiously, felt as if it were back inside her chest where it belonged. Easing her back against a tree trunk, she sat and listened, watching for that strange face, fearing it might abruptly burst through the limbs and brush, grinning its horrible teeth, or worse, that he might come up behind her, reach around the tree trunk with his knife and finish her in a bloody instant. She checked and saw that she still had her purse. She opened it and got hold of the file kit by feel and removed the last file, determined to make better use of it than the first. She had no qualms about using it, knew she would, but what good would it do? The man was obviously stronger than she, and crazy as the pattern in a scratch quilt.

Once again, she thought of Bruce. What would he have done in this situation? He would certainly have been the man for the job. He would have relished it. Would probably have challenged old Moon Face to a one on one at the edge of the mountain, and even with a nail file, would have been confident that he could take him. Ellen thought about how much she hated Bruce, and even now, shed of him, that hatred burned bright. How had she gotten mixed up with that dumb, macho bastard in the first place? He had seemed enticing at first. So powerful. Confident. Capable. The survivalist stuff had always seemed a little nutty, but at first no more nutty than an obsession with golf or a strong belief in astrology.

Perhaps had she known how serious he was about it, she wouldn't have been attracted to him in the first place.

No. It wouldn't have mattered. She had been captivated by him, by his looks and build and power. She had nothing but her own libido and stupidity to blame. And worse yet, when things turned sour, she had stayed and let them sour even more. There had been good moments, but they were quickly eclipsed by Bruce's determination to be ready for the Big Day, as he referred to it. He knew it was coming, if he was somewhat vague on who was bringing it.

But someone would start a war of some sort, a nuclear war, a war in the streets, and only the rugged individualist, well-armed and well-trained and strong of body and will, would survive beyond the initial attack. Those survivors would then carry out guerrilla warfare, hit and run operations, and eventually win back the country from...whoever. And if not win it back, at least have some kind of life free of dictatorship.

It was silly. It was every little boy's fantasy. Living by your wits with gun and knife. And owning a woman. She had been the woman. At first Bruce had been kind enough, treated her with respect. He was obviously on the male chauvinist side, but originally it had seemed harmless enough, kind of Old World charming. But when he moved them to the mountains, that charm had turned to domination, and the small crack in his mental state widened until it was a deep, dark gulf. She was there to keep house and to warm his bed, and any opinions she had contrary to his own were stupid. He read survivalist books constantly and quoted passages to her and suggested she look the books over, be ready to stand tall against the oncoming aggressors.

By the time he had gone completely over the edge, living like a mountain man, ordering her about, his eyes roving from side to side, suspicious of her every move, expecting to hear on his shortwave at any moment World War Three had started, or that race riots were overrunning the USA, or that a shiny probe packed with extraterrestrial invaders brandishing ray guns had landed on the White House lawn, she was trapped in his cabin in the mountains, with him holding the keys to her Chevy and his jeep.

For a time she feared he would become paranoid enough to imagine she was one of the "bad guys" and put a .357 round through her chest. But now she was free of him, escaped from all that...only to be threatened by another man: a moon-faced, silver-toothed monster with a knife.

She returned once again to the question, what would Bruce do, outside of challenging Moon Face in hand-to-hand combat? Sneaking past him would be the best bet, making it back to the Chevy. To do that Bruce would have used guerrilla techniques. "Take advantage of what's at hand," he always said.

Well, she had looked to see what was at hand, and that turned out to be a couple of fingernail files, one of them lost up the mountain. Then maybe she wasn't thinking about this in the right way. She might not be able to outfight Moon Face, but perhaps she could outthink him. She had outthought Bruce, and he had considered himself a master of strategy and preparation. She tried to put herself in Moon Face's head. What was he thinking? For the moment he saw her as his prey, a frightened animal on the run. He might be more cautious because of that trick with the limb, but he'd most likely chalk that one up to accident — which it was for the most part...but what if the prey turned on him?

There was a sudden cracking sound, and Ellen crawled a few feet in the direction of the noise, gently moved aside a limb. Some distance away, discerned faintly through a tangle of limbs, she saw light and detected movement, and knew it was Moon Face. The cracking sound must have been him stepping on a limb. He was standing with his head bent, looking at the ground, flashing a little pocket flashlight, obviously examining the drag path she had made with her hands and knees when she entered into the pine thicket. She watched as his shape and the light bobbed and twisted through the limbs and tree trunks, coming nearer. She wanted to run, but didn't know where.

All right, she thought. All right. Take it easy. Think.

She made a quick decision. Removed the scissors from her purse, took off her shoes and slipped off her pantyhose and put her shoes on again. She quickly snipped three long strips of nylon from her damaged pantyhose and knotted them together, using the sailor knots Bruce had taught her. She cut more thin strips from the hose — all the while listening for Moon Face's approach — and used all but one of them to fasten her fingernail file, point out, securely to the tapered end of one of the small, flexible pine limbs, then she tied one end of the long nylon strip she had made around the limb, just below the file, and crawled backwards, pulling the limb with her, bending it deep. When she had it back as far as she could manage, she took a death grip on the nylon strip, and using it to keep the limb's position taut, crawled around the trunk of a small pine and curved the nylon strip about it and made a loop knot at the base of a sapling that crossed her knee-drag trail. She used her last strip of nylon to fasten to the loop of the knot, and carefully stretched the remaining length across the trail and tied it to another sapling. If it worked correctly, when he came crawling through the thicket, following her, his hands or knees would hit the strip, pull the loop free, and the limb would fly forward, the file stabbing him, in an eye if she were lucky.

Pausing to look through the boughs again, she saw that Moon Face was on his hands and knees, moving through the thick foliage toward her. Only moments were left.

She shoved pine needles over the strip and moved away on her belly, sliding under the cocked sapling, no longer concerned that she might make noise, in fact hoping noise would bring Moon Face quickly. Following the upward slope of the hill, she crawled until the trees became thin again and she could stand. She cut two long strips of nylon from her hose with the scissors, and stretched them between two trees about ankle high.

That one would make him mad if it caught him, but the next one would be the corker.

She went up the path, used the rest of the nylon to tie between two saplings, then grabbed hold of a thin, short limb and yanked at it until it cracked, worked it free so there was a point made from the break. She snapped that over her knee to form a point at the opposite end. She made a quick mental measurement, jammed one end of the stick into the soft ground, leaving a point facing up.

At that moment came evidence her first snare had worked — a loud swishing sound as the limb popped forward and a cry of pain. This was followed by a howl as Moon Face crawled out of the thicket and onto the trail. He stood slowly, one hand to his face. He glared up at her, removed his hand. The file had struck him in the cheek; it was covered with blood. Moon Face pointed his blood-covered hand at her and let out an accusing shriek so horrible she retreated rapidly up the trail. Behind her, she could hear Moon Face running.

The trail curved upward and turned abruptly. She followed the curve a ways, looked back as Moon Face tripped over her first strip and hit the ground, came up madder, charged even more violently up the path. But the second strip got him and he fell forward, throwing his hands out. The spike in the trail hit him low in the throat. She stood transfixed at the top of the trail as he did a pushup and came to one knee and put a hand to his throat. Even from a distance, and with only the moonlight to show it to her, she could see that the wound was dreadful.

Good.

Moon Face looked up, stabbed her with a look, started to rise. Ellen turned and ran. As she made the turns in the trail, the going improved and she theorized that she was rushing up the trail she had originally come down. This hopeful notion was dispelled when the pines thinned and the trail dropped, then leveled off, then tapered into nothing. Before she could slow up, she discovered she was on a sort of peninsula that jutted out from the mountain and resembled an irregular-shaped diving board from which you could leap off into night-black eternity.

In place of the pines on the sides of the trail were numerous scarecrows on poles, and out on the very tip of the peninsula, somewhat dispelling the diving board image, was a shack made of sticks and mud and brambles. After pausing to suck in some deep breaths, Ellen discovered on closer examination that it wasn't scarecrows bordering her path after all. It was people.

There were at least a dozen on either side, placed upright on poles, their feet touching the ground, their knees slightly bent. They were all fully clothed, and in various states of deterioration. Holes had been poked through the backs of their heads to correspond with the hollow sockets of their eyes, and the moonlight came through the holes and shined through the sockets, and Ellen noted, with a warm sort of horror, that one wore a white sun dress and...plastic shoes, and through its head she could see stars. On the corpse's finger was a wedding ring, and the finger had grown thin and withered and the ring was trapped there by knuckle bone alone.

The man next to her was fresher. He too was eyeless and holes had been drilled through the back of his skull, but he still wore glasses and was fleshy. There was a pen and pencil set in his coat pocket. He wore only one shoe. There was a skeleton in overalls, a wilting cigar stuck between his teeth. A fresh-ups man with his cap at a jaunty angle, the moon through his head, and a clipboard tied to his hand with string. His legs had been positioned in such a way it seemed as if he was walking. A housewife with a crumpled, nearly disintegrated grocery bag under her arm, the contents having long fallen through the worn, wet bottom to heap at her feet in a mass of colorless boxes and broken glass. A withered corpse in a ballerina's tutu and slippers, rotting grapefruits tied to her chest with cord to simulate breasts, her legs arranged in such a way she seemed in mid-dance, up on her toes, about to leap or whirl.

The real horror was the children. One pathetic little boy's corpse, still full of flesh and with only his drilled eyes to show death, had been arranged in such a way that a teddy bear drooped from the crook of his elbow. A toy metal tractor and a plastic truck were at his feet. There was a little girl wearing a red rubber clown nose and a propeller beanie. A green plastic purse hung from her shoulder by a strap and a doll's legs had been taped to her palm with black electrician's tape. The doll hung upside down, holes drilled through its plastic head so that it matched its owner.

Things began to click. Ellen understood what Moon Face had been doing down here in the first place. He hadn't been in the Buick when she struck it.

He was disposing of a body. He was a murderer who brought his victims here and set them up on either side of the pathway, parodying the way they were in life, cutting out their eyes and punching through the backs of their heads to let the world in.

Ellen realized numbly that time was slipping away, and Moon Face was coming, and she had to find the trail up to her car. But when she turned to run, she froze. Thirty feet away, where the trail met the last of the pines, squatting dead center in it, arms on his knees, one hand loosely holding the knife, was Moon Face. He looked calm, almost happy, in spite of the fact a large swath of dried blood was on his cheek and the wound in his throat was making a faint whistling sound as air escaped it.

He appeared to be gloating, savoring the moment when he would set his knife to work on her eyes, the gray matter behind them, the bone of her skull.

A vision of her corpse propped up next to the child with the teddy bear, or perhaps the skeletal ballerina, came to mind; she could see herself hanging there, the light of the moon falling through her empty head, melting into the path. Then she felt anger. It boiled inside her. She determined she was not going to allow Moon Face his prize easily. He'd earn it.

Another line from Bruce's books came to her. Consider your alternatives.

She did, in a flash. And they were grim. She could try charging past Moon Face, or pretend to, then dart into the pines. But it seemed unlikely she could make the trees before he overtook her. She could try going over the side of the trail and climbing down, but it was much too steep there, and she'd fall immediately. She could make for the shack and try and find something she could fight with. The last idea struck her as the correct one, the one Bruce would have pursued. What was his quote? "If you can't effect an escape, fall back and fight with what's available to you."

She hurried to the hut, glancing behind her from time to time to check on Moon Face. He hadn't moved. He was observing her calmly, as if he had all the time in the world. When she was about to go through the doorless entryway, she looked back at him one last time. He was in the same spot, watching, the knife held limply against his leg. She knew he thought he had her right where he wanted her, and that's exactly what she wanted him to think. A surprise attack was the only chance she had. She just hoped she could find something to surprise him with.

She hastened inside and let out an involuntary rasp of breath.

The place stank, and for good reason. In the center of the little hut was a folding card table and some chairs, and seated in one of the chairs was a woman, the flesh rotting and dripping off her skull like candle wax, her eyes empty and holes in the back of her head. Her arm was resting on the table and her hand was clamped around an open bottle of whiskey. Beside her, also without eyes, suspended in a standing position by wires connected to the roof, was a man. He was a fresh kill. Big, dressed in khaki pants and shirt and work shoes. In one hand a doubled belt was taped, and wires were attached in such a way that his arm was drawn back as if ready to strike. Wires were secured to his lips and pulled tight behind his head so that he was smiling in a ghoulish way.

Foil gum wrappers were fixed to his teeth, and the moonlight gleaming through the opening at the top of the hut fell on them and made them resemble Moon Face's metal-tipped choppers.

Ellen felt queasy, but fought the sensation down. She had more to worry about than corpses. She had to prevent herself from becoming one. She gave the place a quick pan. To her left was a rust-framed rollaway bed with a thin, dirty mattress, and against the far wall, was a baby crib, and next to that a camper stove with a small frying pan on it. She glanced quickly out the door of the hut and saw that Moon Face had moved onto the stretch of trail bordered by the bodies. He was walking very slowly, looking up now and then as if to appreciate the stars.

Her heart pumped another beat.

She moved about the hut, looking for a weapon.

The frying pan.

She grabbed it, and as she did, she saw what was in the crib. What belonged there. A baby. But dead. A few months old. Its skin thin as plastic and stretched tight over pathetic, little rib bones. Eyes gone, holes through its head. Burnt match stubs between blackened toes. It wore a diaper and the stink of feces wafted from it and into her nostrils. A rattle lay at the foot of the crib. A horrible realization rushed through her. The baby had been alive when taken by this madman, and it had died here, starved and tortured. She gripped the frying pan with such intensity her hand cramped.

Her foot touched something. She looked down. Large bones were heaped there — discarded mommies and daddies, for it now occurred to her that was who the corpses represented. Something gleamed amongst the bones. A gold cigarette lighter. Through the doorway of the hut she saw Moon Face was halfway down the trail. He had paused to nonchalantly adjust the ups man's clipboard. The geek had made his own community here, his own family, people he could deal with — dead people — and it was obvious he intended for her to be part of his creation.

Ellen considered attacking straight-on with the frying pan when Moon Face came through the doorway, but so far he had proven strong enough to take a file in the cheek and a stick in the throat, and despite the severity of the latter wound, he had kept on coming. Chances were he was strong enough to handle her and her frying pan. A back-up plan was necessary. Another one of Bruce's pronouncements. She recalled a college friend, Carol, who used to use her bikini panties to launch projectiles at a teddy bear propped on a chair.

This graduated to an apple on the bear's head. Eventually, Ellen and her dorm sisters got into the act. Fresh panties with tight elastic and marbles for ammunition were ever ready in a box by the door; the bear and an apple were in constant position. In time, Ellen became the best shot of all. But that was ten years ago. Expertise was long gone, even the occasional shot now and then was no longer taken...still...

Ellen replaced the frying pan on the stove, hiked up her dress and pulled her bikini panties down and stepped out of them and picked up the lighter. She put the lighter in the crotch of the panties and stuck her fingers into the leg loops to form a fork and took hold of the lighter through the panties and pulled it back, assured herself the elastic was strong enough to launch the projectile.

All right. That was a start.

She removed her purse, so Moon Face couldn't grab it and snare her, and tossed it aside. She grabbed the whiskey bottle from the corpse's hand and turned and smashed the bottom of it against the cook stove. Whiskey and glass flew. The result was a jagged weapon she could lunge with. She placed the broken bottle on the stove next to the frying pan.

Outside, Moon Face was strolling toward the hut, like a shy teenager about to call on his date. There were only moments left. She glanced around the room, hoping insanely at the last second she would find some escape route, but there was none. Sweat dripped from her forehead and ran into her eye and she blinked it out and half-drew back the panty sling with its golden projectile. She knew her makeshift weapon wasn't powerful enough to do much damage, but it might give her a moment of distraction, a chance to attack him with the bottle. If she went at him straight on with it, she felt certain he would disarm her and make short work of her, but if she could get him off guard...

She lowered her arms, kept her makeshift slingshot in front of her, ready to be cocked and shot.

Moon Face came through the door, ducking as he did, a sour sweat smell entering with him. His neck wound whistled at her like a teapot about to boil. She saw then that he was bigger than she first thought. Tall and broad-shouldered and strong. He looked at her and there was that peculiar expression again. The moonlight from the hole in the roof hit his eyes and teeth, and it was as if that light was his source of energy. He filled his chest with air and seemed to stand a full two inches taller. He looked at the woman's corpse in the chair, the man's corpse supported on wires, glanced at the playpen.

He smiled at Ellen, squeaked more than spoke, "Bubba's home, Sissie."

I'm not Sissie yet, thought Ellen. Not yet.

Moon Face started to move around the card table and Ellen let out a bloodcurdling scream that caused him to bob his head high like a rabbit surprised by headlights. Ellen jerked up the panties and pulled them back and let loose the lighter. It shot out of the panties and fell to the center of the card table with a clunk.

Moon Face looked down at it.

Ellen was temporarily gripped with paralysis, then she stepped forward and kicked the card table as hard as she could. It went into Moon Face, hitting him waist high, startling, but not hurting him.

Now! thought Ellen, grabbing her weapons. Now!

She rushed him, the broken bottle in one hand, the frying pan in the other. She slashed out with the bottle and it struck him in the center of the face and he let out a scream and the glass fractured and a splash of blood burst from him and in that same instant Ellen saw that his nose was cut half in two and she felt a tremendous throb in her hand. The bottle had broken in her palm and cut her. She ignored the pain and as Moon Face bellowed and lashed out with the knife, cutting the front of her dress but not her flesh, she brought the frying pan around and caught him on the elbow, and the knife went soaring across the room and behind the rollaway bed.

Moon Face froze, glanced in the direction the knife had taken. He seemed empty and confused without it. Ellen swung the pan again. Moon Face caught her wrist and jerked her around and she lost the pan and was sent hurtling toward the bed, where she collapsed on the mattress. The bed slid down and smashed through the thin wall of sticks and a foot of the bed stuck out into blackness and the great drop below. The bed tottered slightly, and Ellen rolled off of it, directly into the legs of Moon Face. As his knees bent, and he reached for her, she rolled backwards and went under the bed and her hand came to rest on the knife. She grabbed it, rolled back toward Moon Face's feet, reached out quickly and brought the knife down on one of his shoes and drove it in as hard as she could.

A bellow from Moon Face. His foot leaped back and it took the knife with it. Moon Face screamed, "Sissie! You're hurting me!"

Moon Face reached down and pulled the knife out, and Ellen saw his foot come forward, and then he was grabbing the bed and effortlessly jerking it off of her and back, smashing it into the crib, causing the child to topple out of it and roll across the floor, the rattle clattering behind it.

He grabbed Ellen by the back of her dress and jerked her up and spun her around to face him, clutched her throat in one hand and held the knife close to her face with the other, as if for inspection; the blade caught the moonlight and winked.

Beyond the knife, she saw his face, pathetic and pained and white. His breath, sharp as the knife, practically wilted her. His neck wound whistled softly. The remnants of his nose dangled wet and red against his upper lip and cheek and his teeth grinned a moonlit, metal good-bye.

It was all over, and she knew it, but then Bruce's words came back to her in a rush. "When it looks as if you're defeated, and there's nothing left, try anything."

She twisted and jabbed out at his eyes with her fingers and caught him solid enough that he thrust her away and stumbled backwards. But only for an instant. He bolted forward, and Ellen stooped and grabbed the dead child by the ankle and struck Moon Face with it as if it were a club. Once in the face, once in the midsection. The rotting child burst into a spray of desiccated flesh and innards and she hurled the leg at Moon Face and then she was circling around the rollaway bed, trying to make the door. Moon Face, at the other end of the bed, saw this, and when she moved for the door, he lunged in that direction, causing her to jump back to the end of the bed. Smiling, he returned to his end, waited for her next attempt.

She lurched for the door again, and Moon Face deep-stepped that way, and when she jerked back, Moon Face jerked back too, but this time Ellen bent and grabbed the end of the bed and hurled herself against it. The bed hit Moon Face in the knees, and as he fell, the bed rolled over him and he let go of the knife and tried to put out his hands to stop the bed's momentum. The impetus of the rollaway carried him across the short length of the dirt floor and his head hit the far wall and the sticks cracked and hurtled out into blackness, and Moon Face followed and the bed followed him, then caught on the edge of the drop and the wheels buried up in the dirt and hung there.

Ellen had shoved so hard she fell face down, and when she looked up, she saw the bed was dangling, shaking, the mattress slipping loose, about to glide off into nothingness.

Moon Face's hands flicked into sight, clawing at the sides of the bed's frame.

Ellen gasped. He was going to make it up. The bed's wheels were going to hold. She pulled a knee under her, cocking herself, then sprang forward, thrusting both palms savagely against the bed. The wheels popped free and the rollaway shot out into the dark emptiness.

Ellen scooted forward on her knees and looked over the edge. There was blackness, a glimpse of the mattress falling free, and a pale object, like a whitewashed planet with a great vein of silver in it, jetting through the cold expanse of space. Then the mattress and the face were gone and there was just the darkness and a distant sound like a water balloon exploding. Ellen sat back and took a breather. When she felt strong again and felt certain her heart wouldn't tear through her chest, she stood up and looked around the room. She thought a long time about what she saw. She found her purse and panties, went out of the hut and up the trail, and after a few wrong turns, she found the proper trail that wound its way up the mountainside to where her car was parked. When she climbed over the railing, she was exhausted.

Everything was as it was. She wondered if anyone had seen the cars, if anyone had stopped, then decided it didn't matter. There was no one here now, and that's what was important. She took the keys from her purse and tried the engine. It turned over. That was a relief. She killed the engine, got out and went around and opened the trunk of the Chevy and looked down at Bruce's body. His face looked like one big bruise, his lips were as large as sausages. It made her happy to look at him.

A new energy came to her. She got him under the arms and pulled him out and managed him over to the rail and grabbed his legs and flipped him over the railing and onto the trail. She got one of his hands and started pulling him down the path, letting the momentum help her. She felt good. She felt strong.

First Bruce had tried to dominate her, had threatened her, had thought she was weak because she was a woman, and one night, after slapping her, after raping her, while he slept a drunken sleep, she had pulled the blankets up tight around him and looped rope over and under the bed and used the knots he had taught her, and secured him. Then she took a stick of stove wood and had beat him until she was so weak she fell to her knees. She hadn't meant to kill him, just punish him for slapping her around, but when she got started she couldn't stop until she was too worn out to go on, and when she was finished, she discovered he was dead.

That didn't disturb her much. The thing then was to get rid of the body somewhere, drive on back to the city and say he had abandoned her and not come back. It was weak, but all she had.

Until now.

After several stops for breath, a chance to lie on her back and look up at the stars, Ellen managed Bruce to the hut and got her arms under his and got him seated in one of the empty chairs. She straightened things up as best as she could. She put the larger pieces of the baby back in the crib. She picked Moon Face's knife up off the floor and looked at it and looked at Bruce, his eyes wide open, the moonlight from the roof striking them, showing them to be dull as scratched glass.

Bending over his face, she went to work on his eyes. When she finished with them, she pushed his head forward and used the blade like a drill. She worked until the holes satisfied her. Now if the police found the Buick up there and came down the trail to investigate, and found the trail leading here, saw what was in the shack, Bruce would fit in with the rest of Moon Face's victims. The police would probably conclude Moon Face, sleeping here with his "family," had put his bed too close to the cliff and it had broken through the thin wall and he had tumbled to his death.

She liked it.

She held Bruce's chin, lifted it, examined her work.

"You can be Uncle Brucey," she said, and gave Bruce a pat on the shoulder.

"Thanks for all your advice and help, Uncle Brucey. It's what got me through."

She gave him another pat.

She found a shirt — possibly Moon Face's, possibly a victim's — on the opposite side of the shack, next to a little box of Harlequin Romances, and she used it to wipe the knife, pan, all she had touched, clean of her prints, then she went out of there, back up to her car.

NEIGHBORHOOD WATCH

Joe R. Lansdale is the author of fifty novels and four hundred shorter works, including stories, essays, reviews, film and TV scripts, introductions and magazine articles, as well as a book of poetry. His work has been made into films, Bubba Ho-Tep, Cold In July, as well as the acclaimed TV show, Hap and Leonard. He has also had works adapted to Masters of Horror on Showtime, Netflix's Love, Death and Robots, Shudder's Creepshow. He has written scripts for Batman the Animated Series, and Superman the Animated Series. He has received numerous recognitions for his work. Among them The Edgar for his crime novel The Bottoms. The Spur, for his historical western Paradise Sky. as well as ten Bram Stokers for his horror works. He has also received The Grandmaster Award and the Lifetime Achievement Award from The Horrorwriters Association. Joe has also received the British Fantasy Award, and has had two New York Times Notable Books. He lives in Nacogdoches, Texas with his wife, Karen.

Ted DiLucia is an artist working and living in Rhode Island. He is a graduate of the Rhode Island School of Design.

Our Mission Statement:

Since its founding in August 2012, Crystal Lake Publishing has quickly become one of the world's leading publishers of Dark Fiction and Horror books in print, eBook, and audio formats.While we strive to present only the highest quality fiction and entertainment, we also endeavor to support authors along their writing journey. We offer our time and experience in non-fiction projects, as well as author mentoring and services, at competitive prices. With several Bram Stoker Award wins and many other wins and nominations (including the HWA's Specialty Press Award), Crystal Lake Publishing puts integrity, honor, and respect at the forefront of our publishing operations.

We strive for each book and outreach program we spearhead to not only entertain and touch or comment on issues that affect our readers, but also to strengthen and support the Dark Fiction field and its authors.Not only do we find and publish authors we believe are destined for greatness, but we strive to work with men and women who endeavor to be decent human beings who care more for others than themselves, while still being hard-working, driven, and passionate artists and storytellers. Crystal Lake Publishing is and will always be a beacon of what passion and dedication, combined with overwhelming teamwork and respect, can accomplish. We endeavor to know each and every one of our readers, while building personal relationships with our authors, reviewers, bloggers, podcasters, bookstores, and libraries.

We will be as trustworthy, forthright, and transparent as any business can be, while also keeping most of the headaches away from our authors, since it's our job to solve the problems so they can stay in a creative mind. Which of course also means paying our authors.

We do not just publish books, we present to you worlds within your world, doors within your mind, from talented authors who sacrifice so much for a moment of your time. There are some amazing small presses out there, and through collaboration and open forums we will continue to support other presses in the goal of helping authors and showing the world what quality small presses are capable of accomplishing. No one wins when a small press goes down, so we will always be there to support hardworking, legitimate presses and their authors. We don't see Crystal Lake as the best press out there, but we will always strive to be the best, strive to be the most interactive and grateful, and even blessed press around. No matter what happens over time, we will also take our mission very seriously while appreciating where we are and enjoying the journey. What do we offer our authors that they can't do for themselves through self-publishing?

We are big supporters of self-publishing (especially hybrid publishing), if done with care, patience, and planning. However, not every author has the time or inclination to do market research, advertise, and set up book launch strategies. Although a lot of authors are successful in doing it all, strong small presses will always be there for the authors who just want to do what they do best: write. What we offer is experience, industry knowledge, contacts and trust built up over years. And due to our strong brand and trusting fanbase, every Crystal Lake Publishing book comes with weight of respect. In time our fans begin to trust our judgment and will try a new author purely based on our support of said author. With each launch we strive to fine-tune our approach, learn from our mistakes, and increase our reach. We continue to assure our authors that we're here for them and that we'll carry the weight of the launch and deal with third parties while they focus on their strengths—be it writing, interviews, blogs, signings, etc. We also offer several mentoring packages to authors that include knowledge and skills they can use in both traditional and self-publishing endeavors. We look forward to launching many new careers.This is what we believe in. What we stand for. This will be our legacy.

Welcome to Crystal Lake Publishing—Tales from the Darkest Depths.

THANK YOU FOR PURCHASING THIS BOOK

SLOW SPEED BUMP

CRYSTAL LAKE ENTERTAINMENT

DEAD
END

Printed in the USA
CPSIA information can be obtained
at www.ICGtesting.com
LVHW061128101223
766120LV00009B/72